THE LA!

THE LEGEND OF JAKE JACKSON

GREAT GUNFIGHTERS

BOOK SIX

A WESTERN ADVENTURE

WILLIAM H. JOINER JR.

Copyright © 2020 by William H. Joiner Jr.

Published by DS Productions

ISBN: 9781660723140

DEDICATION

*Gerald Red Elk, old friend and
former high school classmate*

ACKNOWLEDGEMENTS

I am grateful for the constant support of my wife, Tina, and my children, Jacob, Caleb, Sarah and Ainslee.

Thank you to Missy Brewer for editing this book, to Michael Campbell for the book design, and to Bryan Gehrke for the cover artwork.

John 14:6 Jesus answered, "I am the way and the truth and the life. No one comes to the Father except through me."

PREVIOUS PRAISE FROM BESTSELLING AUTHOR
CHEROKEE PARKS

From time to time, an author creates something that takes me back to the days when I was a young cowboy sitting around campfires and bunkhouses listening to the tales of "old timers," some all but unbelievable yet true in every sense of the word, and some pure fancy so far-fetched even a master prevaricator would envy them.

Halfway through *Echoes of the Frontier* I was asking myself if this book was fact or fiction, for the main character, Rowdy Remington, could have been any one of a dozen old cowboys I knew or have heard stories about. I also thought the name of this book could just as easily been *The Making of a Hard Man,* for Rowdy and those who lived during his time had to be hard men just to survive. Yet survive they did, and so much more.

They launched an era of our history that is romanticized and envied to this day, a hundred fifty years later, while living in a harsh landscape doing a nearly impossible job — and making it look simple. Author William H. Joiner, Jr. has captured that time in a nutshell in the telling of Rowdy Remington's life. A man hard when he needs to be, or soft when it's called for, but a man who can see what needs to be done and when, and does it. Not because others will take notice, or to please someone else, but simply because it needs done — no matter how difficult or distasteful.

Bill, I want to thank you personally for sending me back to a time long gone, but a time that is still so much a part of me, by allowing me the opportunity to read this story, and for giving me the high honor of writing a foreword for it. I hope all the fans of Western genre enjoy your work as much as I do.

A NOTE FROM
BESTSELLING AUTHOR
ROBERT HANLON

Those who have had the pleasure of reading the great Westerns Bill Joiner writes—yes I know—many of you already know what I am going to say. Those who have had the pleasure—well let me just cut it short and tell you that he has a great style you'll love. Joiner, to me, is one of those writers who can really get a story across to his audience. He has drive. He's a driven writer—and you'll love this one. It's called "The Legend of Jake Jackson" and it's the kind-of story you've been asking for. Action, gunplay and lots of story. Grab it!

Robert Hanlon – author of the bestselling "Timber: United States Marshal" series, and many other Western adventures.

A NOTE FROM
BESTSELLING AUTHOR
C. WAYNE WINKLE

This tremendous new adventure from William H. Joiner has all those ingredients Western readers enjoy. With plenty of action, gunplay and interplay—this book should find a very receptive fanbase with those who love stories of the Old West. Thank you, William, for continuing to put together some of the best stories of those wonderful Western days!

C. Wayne Winkle – Bestselling author of "Jake Ritter" and many other Western stories.

"Jake Jackson was a legend in the Old West. His ability with a gun was unmatched. His name brought hope to the oppressed and sent shivers of fear up the spines of outlaws. Jake Jackson was equally as revered among the Comanche where he was raised from an infant to become the Comanche Warrior, White Wolf. There were many songs sung around campfires in Comanche villages praising his fierceness in battle.

Jake Jackson could revert back to his Comanche ways in the blink of an eye when the situation demanded no mercy to those preying on the weak or unprotected."

Caleb Burk asked Jake in private, "Pa, I'm 15 now. I love Ma and Grandpa, but I no longer want to be left behind. I want to be a warrior like you. Red Elk believed you were ready to be a warrior. When will you believe that I am ready?"

Jake replied, "The ways of the white man are different than the Comanche. A Comanche woman was raised knowing and accepting Indian ways. What is normal for a Comanche is difficult for your Ma. She doesn't understand it. There is a rite of passage for a Comanche boy to be accepted as a warrior in the tribe." Caleb Burk nodded, "I am ready for the rite of passage. When can we start?" Jake grinned. He joked, "We may have to tomahawk your Ma first." Jake and Caleb Burk laughed.

That night at the supper table, Jake stated, "I believe it is time for Caleb Burk to go through the rite of passage to become a Comanche warrior." Anne exclaimed, "What? When was all this decided? Caleb Burk is not a Comanche! Why would he need to do this rite of passage?" Anne was afraid. She had seen Jake transform to the Comanche warrior, White Wolf on several occasions. Anne didn't want her son to ever be that savage.

Jake continued, "I have raised Caleb Burk in the way of the Comanche. I have taught him like Red Elk taught me. I have sensed that Caleb Burk had a connection to the Comanche when he was born. Caleb Burk is not ashamed to be white, but he is drawn to the Comanche."

Caleb Burk said to Anne, "Ma, what Pa is saying is true. Whenever he tells me about bring brought up in the Comanche village, it makes me want to be there myself. Sometimes I feel there's a part of me missing." Anne asked Jake, "What exactly is this rite of passage?" Jake responded,

"The boy is given a buffalo robe, a bone pipe, tobacco and a flint rock to make fire. I will take him where I did my rite of passage in the Wichita Mountains. He will stay there for four days praying and fasting. The Great Spirit will give him a vision that will guide him for the rest of his life."

The color drained from Anne's face, "Four days? That's a long time. How will he be protected?" Jake replied, "A man must learn to protect himself." Burk Burnett chimed in, "What about guns? Can he take a gun with him?" Jake shook his head, "No weapons."

From the looks on her husband's and son's faces, Anne knew any further protests would be a lost cause. Anne sighed and muttered, "I didn't sign up to be an Indian." Later Burk Burnett whispered to Caleb Burk, "Don't worry, boy. I'll stash one of by good Colts in that robe." His grandson grinned, "Sorry, Grandpa. I can't accept it. The rite of passage must be the Comanche way." Burk Burnett scowled, "You might wish you had a sixshooter if a pack of wolves get to biting on your ass!"

When Jake and Caleb Burk arrived at the place where Jake went through his rite of passage high in the Wichita Mountains, Jake smiled at the remembrance of the vision the Great Spirit gave him. The white wolf with sharp fangs was vivid in his memory.

No words were exchanged between Jake and his son. Jake rode off leading Caleb Burk's horse. Caleb Burk gathered up the robe, pipe, tobacco and flint. He built a small fire, sat cross-legged on the robe and waited on his vision from the Great Spirit. By the third day, Caleb Burk had smoked the tobacco. Fasting had prepared his mind for the spiritual.

As he slept that night, Caleb Burk dreamed of a great white bear standing on his hind legs and snapping his jaws. When Caleb Burk was jolted from his sleep, he searched for the bear. When he did not find it, Caleb Burk realized the white bear was the vision given to him by the Great Spirit.

The two men watched the young boy from their concealment behind an outcropping of rocks. One remarked, "Looks like we got us a little pilgrim. That buffalo robe ought to bring a pretty penny. Might buy us enough whiskey for a week!"

Duane Carney and John Featherston met in the jail at Ft. Smith Arkansas. They immediately struck up a friendship due to common interests. Duane remarked, "You know what really pisses me off, John? Some folks are so high and mighty cause they got more than me. It ain't my fault they got lucky and I didn't. And do you think the sum bitches might be willing to share?...Nah, they want to act like they done outworked me or some such!"

John spit, "I knowed exactly what you mean! I got the same buzzard's luck! People want to look down their noses cause I like to drinks a bit. It makes me want to take em down a peg or two...Once we get out of this hoosegow, me and you oughta partner up. We'll show them sum bitches what for!"

Duane cackled as he stuck out his hand, "Put er there, pard! Maybe our luck has finally changed!" The sheriff and his deputy were listening in the next room. The sheriff declared, "I've had my fill of feeding them two saddle tramps. Most folks would realize they're in jail. Those two act like this is a hotel. Run em out of town!" The deputy responded, "Sheriff, neither one has a horse. You want me to put them on foot?" The sheriff replied, "I durn sure do!

3

You make sure they understand that if I ever see them back in Ft. Smith, I'll put a bullet in their gizzard!"

As they started walking, John complained, "Well, ain't this the double-barrel shits! No horse and no whiskey. I can't catch a break!" Duane held up a hand, "Did you hear that?...I swear it sounded like a jackass…If it is, we might save some boot leather after all."

When they got close enough, Duane and John saw two jackasses penned in a corral. The farmhouse was a dilapidated old shack. John whispered, "Our luck just keeps getting better and better. I wonder if who lives there might have any biscuits or whiskey?" An old man with a cane hobbled out the door. He shouted, "I seen you two old coots sneaking around! Get off my property! You ain't got no business here!" Earl Henderson was known as a cantankerous oldtimer, but harmless. Most thought he was all bark but no bite.

Duane muttered, "Who's he calling an old coot?" John responded, "Howdy neighbor! We're just a little down on our luck. We was hoping you might have a chore or two that we could trade for a few biscuits? We're powerful hungry." The old man frowned, "I ain't running no old folks home. Get gone before I have to sic the law on you!"

John kept walking. He cupped his hand to his ear, "What's that, mister? I don't hear so good no more." Earl yelled, "Are you deef? I said get!" To the frustration of the old man, John walked all the way to him. Earl began to shake his fist when John grabbed his cane. John started beating the old man with his own cane. As blood ran from the wounds on his head, Earl put up his hands to shield himself. He begged "Stop, mister. You can have whatever I got. Just don't hit me no more." John snorted, "You shoulda thought about that before you went to running your mouth!"

John quit long enough to see how his new partner was taking his assault. Duane waited for an opening, then began kicking the old man, "You ain't so tough now, is you?" A bloodied Earl lay motionless. Duane asked, "Is he dead?" John replied, "Close enough. First let's see if the old man's got any vittles. Then we'll check for some whiskey!" Duane responded, "To hell with that! Let's see about the whiskey first!"

Duane found a bottle of rot-gut that was half empty. He and John traded swigs until it was gone. John exclaimed, "Why, looky here! The old man's still got a most of a pan of biscuits from his breakfast. That bacon looks good too!" After wolfing down the food, the outlaws ransacked the house and the broken down barn. They stole an old pistol, half a box of cartridges and a few dollars that Earl had hidden in the sugar bowl. Before leaving, John toed Earl's body, "Yep, he's dead. His mouth done him in!"

There wasn't any saddles or bridles, so the killers rigged up two rope bridles. Duane dragged the body inside and set fire to the house. He explained, "This way, when they find him, the body's burned up. They'll think the fire is what killed him." John retorted, "I got me a partner that's a genius! Good work, pard." Duane and John mounted the jackasses and trotted south.

Duane and John watched Caleb Burk a little longer. Finally, Duane whispered, "What are we waiting on? It's just a dang kid. Let's kill him and take that robe. We ain't had no whiskey in a week. I feel like I'm in Hell. I need me some whiskey." The killers were careful about the path they took down to the boy. They crawled silently for a spell. When

John cautiously peered over the last rock between them and their victim, he was astonished to see the kid was nowhere to be seen.

John reached down and lifted Duane up to confirm what he was seeing. John said softly, "Where'd he go? The buffalo robe is still there…Where'd the little sum bitch go?" Duane scratched his head, "I got no idee!" Something slammed John to the ground, sending his pistol clattering across the rocks. One blow from the rock put out the lights in John's eyes. Duane was slow to react to what was happening. The same rock caved in the side of his head.

The next day when Jake came to retrieve Caleb Burk, Jake was concerned to see buzzards circling over the spot where he left his son. Jake heeled Buck into a gallop. He was relieved to see Caleb Burk sitting on his robe. The buzzards were pecking at the two bodies nearby. Jake also saw the fresh scalps tied to the bone pipe.

Jake dismounted, squatting next to his son waiting for an explanation. Caleb Burk stated, "Pa, the Great Spirit gave me my vision. It was a great white bear standing on his hind legs. He looked like he was ready to do battle." Jake smiled, "That's good, son. I am White Wolf. You are White Bear. Your medicine may be stronger than mine." Caleb Burk shrugged, "Maybe, Pa. I just don't see how I could be a greater warrior than you. That's not possible."

Father and son sat quietly for a while until Jake nodded towards the bodies and asked, "What about those two? What's their story?" Caleb Burk said matter of factly, "They tried to kill me. I killed them. I think they may have wanted my robe." Jake added, "And the scalps?" Caleb Burk smiled, "I didn't have a knife, but one of them did. The pipe was the only thing I could think to attach them to."

Jake and Caleb Burk sat in silence for a while longer. Jake said, "You know you can't take those scalps home...If you did, there might be a third scalp added to them. Caleb Burk grinned, "I know, Pa...but lifting the hair of my enemies made me feel that I really was a Comanche warrior." Jake put a hand on his son's shoulder, "A true Comanche doesn't look for an excuse to kill. If he is attacked, he does kill. You are a true Comanche, my son."

When father and son got back to the ranch, Anne and Burk Burnett wanted to hear everything. Caleb Burk explained, "The Great Spirit gave me my spirit vision. It is a white bear." He didn't tell his Ma or Grandpa about the two men who tried to kill him. Caleb Burk knew it was wise to keep that information to himself, especially about the scalping. Jake and Caleb Burk never discussed the scalps again.

Later after Burk Burnett made sure that Jake and Anne were out of earshot, he asked, "I bet you wished you had one of my good Colts when them wolves got to howling at night? Got to thinking about them teeth sinking into your ass, didn't you?" Caleb Burk laughed, "No, Grandpa. I was never afraid of the wolves. My spirit animal is a bear. Bears aren't scared of wolves." Burk Burnett sighed, "You're gonna end up a durn Comanche just like your Pa. If you start scalping folks, your Ma will probably scalp you." Caleb Burk choked back another laugh.

That night when they were in bed, Anne spoke softly, "Caleb Burk is different. He's not the same boy who left here a few days ago...He seems less like a boy, more like a man." Jake replied, "That's the whole purpose of the rite of passage. Having the Great Spirit give a boy his vision, will change the boy." Anne sniffed, "Maybe so...I don't think I like it."

Chico Ramirez was born on a small farm near Santo Domingo, Mexico. The local Federales were crooked. They squeezed the people with a fake tax. They would change the tax if they thought someone could afford it. Capt. Ortega always said, "Sometimes it may not be much, but everyone pays the tax."

Chico's father, Jose and mother, Maria scratched out a living with a small corn patch, planted in the rocky soil. When Chico was 7, Capt. Ortega ordered Jose, "Ramirez, you are doing well here. Your farm seems very prosperous. My expenses are increasing every day. I have no choice but to double your tax. I'm sure you understand." Jose choked, "But...but Capitan. I barely have enough to feed my family. I cannot pay a bigger tax!" Ortega smirked, "You must pay. Everyone pays. You will find a way."

Jose managed to pay the additional tax for the first two weeks. That took all his money. The third week Jose told Capt. Ortega, "I cannot pay the tax. I need a little more time." Ortega would not relent, "I am truly sorry you can't pay, but everyone must pay." He commanded the sergeant, "Hang him." Maria screamed as the soldiers dragged Jose to a large cottonwood. They tied his hands behind his back, looped the rope over a strong limb and slipped the noose over Jose's head.

Maria pleaded, "Capt. Ortega, please, you mustn't do this! My husband is a fine man. I beg you. Don't do this!" Ortega shrugged, "Everyone must pay...Sergeant." The sergeant dallied the rope around his saddle horn. He spurred his horse, lifting Jose off the ground. As Jose kicked in a frantic attempt at finding his footing, Maria grabbed his legs trying to lift him up. She was crying hysterically, "Jose!...Jose!"

When Jose quit struggling, Maria seized his hoe and charged Capt. Ortega. As she raised the hoe, Ortega shot the woman in the heart. Maria swayed momentarily before collapsing in death. Young Chico had watched in a daze as both his parents were murdered before his eyes.

Capt. Ortega told Chico, "You can stay here and farm the corn, but you have to pay the tax. If you choose not to pay the tax like your Papa did, I will hang you too. Everyone pays the tax!" Chico snuck away in the night. He walked to his Uncle's farm, over one hundred miles away. During the long journey Chico vowed, "I will return one day, Capitan. You and your sergeant will pay for killing Papa and Mama."

His Uncle Pedro was devastated at the news of the deaths of Jose and Maria. He told Chico, "You are welcome here, hijo. My wife and I could not have children. We will love you as our own son." Chico grew up tall and strong. Unfortunately, the loss of his parents at such a young age, twisted Chico's heart. He had no compassion, showing cruelty even to animals. Uncle Pedro tried to help, but was ignored by Chico, "Hijo, that donkey did nothing to you. You should not hit him with a stick." Chico shrugged, "He is not moving fast enough."

When Chico turned 15, he left his Uncle's house in the middle of the night. Chico never told his uncle or his aunt goodbye. In fact he never saw them again. Chico didn't hate his Uncle Pedro. It was just that he had no more use for him. When Chico no longer needed someone, he left them behind. Chico felt that goodbyes were a waste of time.

Chico packed enough food for the trek back to his old home. He also carried a sickle that was used to cut barley for harvest, Chico cut off most of the handle so the sickle could be wielded with one hand. Capt. Ortega was asleep between two whores in the back room of the cantina. Both whores were passed out drunk. They were snoring loud enough to mask any noise that Chico made. Chico rolled the closest whore off the bed. She landed on the floor with a small thud. She never stopped snoring.

Chico pressed the sharp edge of the sickle against Ortega's throat. Chico whispered in his ear, "Capitan, I have returned like I promised you the day you hung Papa and shot Mama. Wake up. I don't want you to sleep through this." The sting of the blade cutting into the jowls of his neck caused Capt. Ortega to awaken. In the haze of his drunken stupor, Ortega slowly became conscious. He muttered, "What?...What is this?"

A fleeting moment of recognition flashed in his eyes. Capt. Ortega watched in horror as the sickle was raised then brought down swiftly. Chico laughed as the severed head separated from the body. No one knew of the execution until the first whore sobered up, wiped the drool off her chin and began to scream at the blood that covered her body.

Chico stole the Captain's pistola, some pesos that were laying on the table by the bed and his fine white horse that was tied up in front of the cantina. Chico was waiting in an alley outside of the cantina for the fat sergeant to show up. The sergeant was shaken awake by one of the Federales, "Sergeant, Capt. Ortega has been murdered in his sleep! You must come quickly!" When the fat sergeant waddled by his position, Chico heeled his horse to block the sergeant's path.

Chico sneered, "Do you remember me, Sergeant? You hung my Papa for being poor!" The sergeant was confused at seeing the boy riding Capt. Ortega's horse. Chico snorted, "You are probably too stupid to remember me!" Chico put three slugs into the sergeant's ample belly. Chico laughed as he rode off. He knew the Federale's death would be certain but painful.

The realization that killing two Federales would cause the Mexican army to send patrols looking for him, made Chico decide to head to the Rio Grande. He thought he had a significantly better chance at not being arrested by escaping into the United States. Chico told his new horse, "The gringos do not care about a couple of dead Mexicans. I will be safe there."

Chico approached the two cowboys herding cattle. He asked, "I have a fine horse to sell. Would you like to buy him?" One of the cowboys furrowed his brow, "Messican, you ain't fooling nobody! That ain't your horse! Who did you steal him from?" Chico lied, "I found him, senor. I looked for his owner, but did not see anyone." The second cowboy laughed, "That's the biggest bunch of horseshit I ever heared! I reckon you killed the sum bitch who owned him!" Chico spun the horse around, taking off at a gallop." Both cowboys laughed as Chico disappeared from sight.

The cowboys were still laughing as they sipped coffee over the campfire that night. Zeke stated, "Surely that Messican boy didn't think we was gonna pay him good money for a stolen horse." Bob replied, "I will say he had some sand…especially for a Messican." The flames from the muzzle of the pistol leapt out of the darkness. It was closely followed by a loud bang. Zeke doubled over clutching his stomach. Bob was stunned, "What the hell…" The second shot struck Bob in the back of the head. Zeke was sprinkled with Bob's blood.

Chico stepped out of the shadows. Zeke pleaded, "Now hold on there, boy. I love Messicans. Some of my best friends are Messicans. They is some fine people." Chico smirked, "Gringo, you are a worse liar than even me." Chico triggered his pistola. The slug slammed into Zeke's face, killing him instantly.

Chico boasted as he looked around, "All my life I have been poor. Now I am rich! I own three horses, many guns and the money the gringos have. Why should I work under the hot sun when I can take what I want from the rich!" Chico outfitted himself from the spare clothes from the cowboys' saddle bags. Bob's boots fit him perfectly. Their hats were the worst for wear due to being splattered with blood from the execution of Zeke and Bob. Chico decided to stick with his sombrero.

There was a cantina located in a trading post situated on the Texas side of its border with New Mexico. The cantina was operated by Rosa Sanchez. In an area noted for ruthless men, no one expected that a woman would be the most cut-throat of all. Rosa ruled the cantina with a hatred for gringos and men in general. There was no sign outside, but the bar was commonly called Rosa's Cantina. White men quickly learned to avoid the cantina. Rumor said that the last white man that entered was staked out spread-eagled. Rosa sliced open his stomach and let her pigs feed on his entrails.

Rosa had bought two young white women from the Comancheros. She told them on their first day on the job, "You will do what I say when I say it! You will let anyone use you in however it pleases them long as I approve it. Your pay will be tortillas and water. All pesos go to me! If you try to escape, I will rip open your belly and let the pigs finish you off!"

Rosa eyed the stranger suspiciously. She demanded, "What do you want?" The young Mexican boy replied, "Tequila." Rosa responded, "Do you have money to pay?" Chico said, "I have Mexican pesos and American dollars. What would you like?" Rosa smiled, "And where did a young boy get so much money?" Chico declared, "I killed gringos for it. That's the way I get money." At first Rosa had a look of disbelief. She burst out laughing, "You must be a hombre muy malo!"

Chico reached across the bar and helped himself to a bottle of Tequila, "How much? Talking makes me thirsty." It was a rare moment for Rosa. She was speechless at the brazenness of this boy. Rosa looked at an astonished Edgar. Edgar had murdered and robbed so many people, he could not remember them all. His black eye patch and the jagged scar down his face, testified that some of Edgar's victims had fought back. Rosa grinned, "Edgar, what do you think. You think little Pepito has killed many men?" Edgar removed the stub of a cigar from the corner of his mouth, "I don't think he can kill the flies off his own ass!"

Rosa and the dozen banditos in the cantina all laughed uproariously. Rosa asked, "What about it, Pepito? Do you think you could kill such a man as Edgar?" As Edgar smirked at Rosa, taking his eyes off Chico, Chico drew his sixgun and fired at point-blank range. The bullet slammed into Edgar's chest causing him to fall backwards, tipping over the stool he was sitting on.

The loud bang stunned Rosa and the onlookers. She finally said to Chico, "You killed him! You shot Edgar!" Chico shrugged, "I didn't say I wouldn't kill Mexicans.

Although I would rather kill gringos." Chico paused before going on, "Anyone else you would like me to kill?"

Rosa had a healthy respect for Edgar, but it never reached the level of fear. For the first time since she had been abused as a child at the hands of her own father, Rosa felt the icy hand of fear grip her heart. She said in a shaky voice, "Pepito, I may have misjudged you. You are a hombre malo." Chico replied calmly, "My name is not Pepito. It is Chico...Chico Ramirez."

Rosa nervously said to a couple of dazed banditos, "Drag Edgar out of here. You do not have to bury him. Give him to my pigs. They have not eaten for a few days. When the men tossed Edgar's body over the fence into the pig pen, the pigs attacked the body slashing with their tusks. In seconds blood and entrails were flying in the air. Even the two hardened outlaws recoiled in horror.

As her two bar girls ducked their heads in shame, Rosa leaned over from behind the bar exposing her ample bosom, "Anything I can do for you, Senor Ramirez?" Chico stared for a minute down the low-cut blouse before shaking his head, "Not now...maybe later."

Chico had never experienced a woman before. Rosa was his first introduction. Down through the years, Rosa had learned to use her body as the quickest way to gain power over a man. Despite what most of the men thought, Rosa cared nothing for any of them. At the first opportunity she wouldn't hesitate to use any man for pig fodder.

Rosa purred lying next to Chico in her bed as the sunlight crept into her room, "Senor, you were magnificent last night. I have been waiting all my life for a man such as yourself! What can I do for you?" Chico began putting on his clothes.

He responded, "I need some men to become part of my gang. They must know how to use a gun and knife. My men should not be afraid to do at what needs to be done. I will pay them from what we steal from the gringos."

Chico sat down at a table of three men. One man said, "Rosa said you wanted to see us. She said that there was mucho dinero for us. Is this true?" Chico responded, "I will pay well for the right men. I need men who aren't women. I hate gringos, but we will take from Mexicans too." Juan, Luis and Josie exchanged glances. Juan declared, "I will join you, Chico. I want to be rich." Luis nodded, "Count me in too." Only Josie hesitated before speaking, "I like the idea except why are you the patron? All of us have more experience than you. I think we should vote on who leads us."

Chico smiled, "There is one good reason why I should be the patron." Josie smirked, "And why is that?" Chico pulled his gun and fired in one smooth motion. The .45 slug slammed into Josie's skull at close range. It appeared his head exploded. Blood, skull fragments and gray brain matter scattered around the room. Chico held the smoking gun level, "Any other questions about who is the patron?" Juan and Luis quickly shook their heads no.

Rosa giggled, "My pigs are going to get fat!" Half a dozen of the banditos scurried to take Josie's body to the pig pen. Watching Rosa's pigs eat men was entertaining. The act had become popular with the low-lifes who occupied the cantina. A few nights earlier one of the renegades suddenly shot another who was seated at the same table. He exclaimed, "Let's feed the pigs!...Besides I didn't like this sum bitch much anyways!" The men started watching each other. None wanted to be sacrificed to be that night's entertainment.

As they waited for the stagecoach, Juan asked Chico, "Should we pull our bandannas up to hide our faces?" Chico sneered, "Masks aren't needed. Dead men can't testify." The outlaws lay in wait just around a bend in the road. The coach would have to slow to make the turn. It was the perfect spot for an ambush.

As the passengers climbed into the stagecoach, 4 year old Oliver exclaimed, "Pa, this is my first stagecoach ride!" E.H. Adrain smiled, "My first one too, son. I'm glad I got to share it with you." Abigail straightened up Oliver's clothes, "Uncle Dan and Aunt Linda are going to be so glad to see you!"

E.H. and his wife, Abigail had left their dry goods store in Ft. Worth in the capable hands of Millie Strand to visit Abigail's sister and husband in San Angelo. Millie had worked for the Adrains' for over five years and knew the store as well as they did. Even though they were the only passengers, Abigail insisted they all sit together on one side of the coach. She sat in the middle where she could hold the hands of her husband and her son.

As he slowed the coach, the driver alerted the guard, "I hate this stretch of the road. It always makes the hair stand up on the back of my neck. It's made to order for a robbery! Cock that old shotgun. That sound makes me feel better." Ed spit a stream of tobacco juice. He grinned, "Luther, you getting scary in your old age? As long as I got ol' Betsy here, we ain't got nothing to worry about!" Ed spit again.

The first shot resulted in a bullet banging into Ed's throat. The slug severed Ed's spinal cord causing his head to dangle limply to one side. Ol' Betsy clattered harmlessly into the coach's boot. Luther slapped the reins on the horses' backs urging them to move faster. Another blast from Chico's gun

16

sent a bullet burrowing into one of the horse's ribs. The horse squealed as it went down with its legs thrashing.

The stagecoach was dangerously close to turning over. As it teetered, Luther swore, "Damn it all to hell…" The coach tipped over landed on its side and slid for as long as the three horses could pull it and the dead horse. The out-of-control team of horses were quieted by a barrage of bullets.

Luther was stunned when he was thrown to the ground. When he was able to refocus, he was staring down the muzzle of a pistol. Luther saw the flame burst out of the muzzle, but he never heard blast of the gun or felt the slug slamming into his brain. Chico laughed, "Gringos are so easy to kill!"

Luis had scampered to the top of the stagecoach laying on its side. He pried open the door and ordered the three passengers, "Come out! You will be safe if you give up without a fight!" E.H. shouted, "It's just me, my wife and my boy! We'll come out peaceably! You won't get any trouble from us!" E.H. gingerly climbed out and helped Abigail and Oliver down.

Chico was eagerly counting the money from the mail pouch that was retrieved from the coach's boot. He looked up long enough to order Luis and Juan, "You know what to do. I should not have to tell you twice!" Juan plucked the money that was hidden in the inside pocket of E.H.'s coat. Juan calmly executed E.H. with a bullet to the back of his head. Luis shot little Oliver in the same manner.

Abigail fainted from the shock of witnessing her husband and son murdered. Luis asked, "Chico, you said we could use any woman that we captured. Can we still do that?" Chico nodded, "Just a little. Do not damage her. She is worth mucho dinero. I will sell her to Rosa." When the renegades were finished with Abigail, they were joking. Luis said, "She was good, but I still like a good sturdy Mexican woman the best!" Juan laughed, "I don't think you care as long as you have one under you…"

All the outlaws dove for cover at the unexpected sound of the gunshot. Abigail had slipped Luis's gun from his holster. She quickly cocked it and stuck the barrel in her mouth before pulling the trigger. When Chico realized what had happened, he swore, "Damn you, Luis! You just cost me money!" Chico drew his sixgun and shot Luis between the eyes. Chico was still cursing Luis when he and Juan rode away with their loot. They left behind three dead innocent victims, four dead horses and one dead outlaw for the buzzards and coyotes.

Over time Chico added more men to his gang. He now had ten of the worst dregs of human society riding with him. One night Rosa made a suggestion, "Chico, Hermosa, since I help you get the men for your jobs, don't you think it is fair to give me a cut?...And that's not all I do for you. Don't I always make sure you are warm and fed?"

After giving it some thought, Chico smiled, "I think you are right, Rosa. I know how much you love men. Tonight you will service all my men…for free. That should make you happy!" The worst part for Rosa was not the individual physical acts. It was pretending that she enjoyed it. Rosa was terrified that Chico would feed her to her own pigs.

Chico struck a partnership with a band of Comancheros. Their leader went by the name, Lopez. Chico thought he looked more Indian than Mexican. Lopez told Chico, "I will buy whatever you steal…cattle, horses, women…anything of value. You can count on your good friend Lopez, to give

18

you the best price!" The men shook hands and slapped each other's backs in a fake show of friendship. Neither trusted the other.

Chico sent three of his men out separately to scout for victims who could fatten his larder. One scout returned with a favorable report, "Patron, there is a ranch close to the Mexican border that has many cows and only three cowboys to protect it. We could kill the men easily. Then drive the cattle to Lopez for a quick sale!"

A scowl spread over Chico's face, "Did I ask you to plan the raid? Your job is to find opportunities! I do not need your ideas!" The scout began to sweat as he envisioned hog tusks penetrating his throat. He knelt, "I am sorry, Patron! It won't happen again!" Since the scout did bring news of an easy robbery, Chico allowed him to live.

Chico studied the comings and goings of the cowboys on the small ranch. The scout had been correct about everything but one. There was a fourth person on the ranch, but it was an old woman who probably cooked for the men. Chico didn't consider her a threat so the raid would go on as planned.

Kenton and Martha Dickerson had been married for 40 years. The first 20 were spent in Austin. They met when they were both clerking at a large mercantile store. After they wed, Kenton became more and more frustrated with what he considered "city" life. Kenton said, "Honey, there are too many folks already in Austin. More just keep coming every day. I want to go back to my roots. I was raised on a ranch. I know how to tend cattle. I've got a good mind to take what money we have and buy a small ranch. I don't know that I can take this much longer!" Martha smiled, "Whatever you say. I love you dearly. My place is with you. I will follow you anywhere."

Despite trying but not having any children, the Dickersons were satisfied with their life on the ranch in south Texas. Life on the frontier is hard on women. Martha aged prematurely. If Kenton noticed, he never said anything. Kenton told Martha repeatedly, "Honey, you're a pretty as a new-born calf!" Down through the years Kenton added two cowhands, Clem and Robert. Both were aging, down-on-their luck cowboys. They were grateful that Kenton hired them on. There was very little cash, but the men lived in the old house with Kenton and Martha. Martha kept them well fed. They were considered family.

Chico waited until the sun was up. Kenton, Clem and Robert had finished the breakfast that Martha fixed of bacon, biscuits, beef and buttermilk. The men were saddling their horses for the day. Martha was cleaning up the kitchen.

Chico screamed an Apache war cry as he and his gang boiled up out of an arroyo that was close to the house. Clem and Robert initially froze in confusion. They pulled their pistols and started returning the gunfire. Robert shouted, "Kill them sum bitches!" It was over quickly for Clem and Robert. Bullets pelted their bodies. Even though they were dead on their feet, Clem and Robert continued to jerk in response to the slugs that were striking them. Mercifully, the old cowboys collapsed into the peacefulness of death.

Kenton's first response was thoughts of Martha. Disregarding his own safety, Kenton ran to the house with bullets nipping at his clothes. He yelled, "Martha! Martha! Are you alright?" Martha had flattened herself on the floor at the first sounds of the attack. She had survived several

Indian raids. Martha knew what to expect. Martha replied, "I'm fine. Keep your head down!"

As Kenton took a position by a window. He began shooting at the renegades. Martha crawled across the floor dragging Kenton's old rifle. She looked up at her kneeling husband, "Clem and Robert?" Kenton shook his head, "Goners." Martha asked, "What are our odds at making it?" Kenton frowned, "Not good. I've killed a couple. There's just too many of them!"

Martha was silent for a minute before saying, "We done talked about this. When the time comes I expect you to do what we agreed on!" Martha closed her eyes to make it easier on Kenton. They had agreed there was a fate worse than death. Kenton had sworn he would never let that happen to his beloved wife. When Kenton was down to his last two bullets, through his tears he fired one of them into Martha's head. He placed the muzzle of his sixgun against his temple. His last slug sent him to be reunited with Martha.

Chico had lost two men. He felt that was a small price to pay for 300 cattle. Chico left the former gang members where they lay. They no longer mattered. One of the other outlaws started to ask about the fallen gang members, "What about..." He didn't finish due to second thoughts about his patron's response to his question.

Two of the cowhands for the massive Four-Sixes ranch were patrolling its southern border looking for strays. Chico and his banditos were driving the stolen herd across Four-Sixes land headed to west Texas to sell them to the Comancheros. Cline and Nathan sat on their horses on a ridge watching the cattle drive. Cline furrowed his brow, "Nathan, there's something about them cows and the ol' boys herding them that don't seem right. What do you think?" Nathan pulled off his hat and scratched his head, "I reckon I'm thinking the same thing you are." Cline added, "Well that's our land. Let's go find out who's on it."

Cline said to the first drover they approached, "Do you know you are on the Four-Sixes ranch?" The outlaw turned up his hands as he shrugged, pretending not to understand English. Cline demanded, "Who's the ramrod for this outfit?" At that time Chico rode up, "How can I help you, amigo?" An irritated and suspicious Nathan interjected, "You got a bill of sale for theses cows?"

Two other renegades had drifted over to the pow-wow. Chico smiled at the Four-Sixes cowboys. He ordered his men in Spanish, "Kill the gringos!" Cline and Nathan understood Spanish. They grabbed for their pistols. Chico already had his gun leveled. He began to fire. Chico was quickly joined by the other three banditos. Cline and Nathan barely cleared leather before being cut down by a hail of bullets.

After making sure the cowboys were dead, Chico commanded, "Leave the gringos for the buzzards. We must hurry to get our money from the Comancheros. Double the pace of the herd!"

Three days later Sandy Young who was next in command behind Jake on the ranch, rode up to the big house one night. Jake, Burk, Anne and Caleb Burke were seated on the porch enjoying the night breezes before bed. It was obvious by the look on Sandy's face there was trouble. Burk questioned, "What is it, Sandy? What's wrong?" Sandy had his hat in his hand. He said dejectedly, "It's Cline and Nathan...they're dead. They was killed by rustlers."

Burk bolted up out of his chair. He demanded, "How?" Sandy continued, "I wasn't too worried about them because they was riding the south pastures. Sometimes it takes a few days to get that done. This morning me and some of the boys went looking for them. The circling buzzards led us to their bodies. They were already in such bad shape, we buried them there."

Jake asked, "Sandy, what do you think happened?" Sandy replied, "There was a herd of cattle being driven across our land. I figured Cline and Nathan got into a dustup over it. The rustlers shot them." Sandy paused, "Do you want me to take a few of the men and go after them? I'd of already done it, but I figured I needed to let y'all know what had happened." Jake responded, "Thanks but that's more in my line of work. I'll leave at daylight in the morning."

There was a strained silence after Sandy went to the bunkhouse. Caleb Burk stated, "Pa, it's time." Anne's heart was gripped by the icy hand of fear. She was terrified that the day she dreaded the most was finally here. Jake shrugged, "Maybe it is time, son." Anne jumped from her chair and screamed, "No, it's not time! It's time for our boy to be a boy! He's too young! I'm putting my foot down on all this Comanche foolishness! Caleb Burk is not going with you!"

Burk and Caleb Burk stared at the floor neither one daring to look at Anne. Jake softly replied to his wife, "Anne, I was younger than Caleb Burk when Red Elk took me on my first raiding party. He expected me to be a man so he treated me like a man. The only man I know who can ride and shoot better than our son, is me." Anne burst into tears. She ran sobbing into their bedroom, slamming the door behind her. Caleb Burk looked questioningly at Jake. Jake said, "Let her be. Deep down she knows it's time for you to be a man. She just needs a little time."

Later when Jake climbed into bed, Anne reached for his hand and pulled it to her lips. Jake rolled over to face her, covering her hand with his. Jake kissed his wife on the forehead. He whispered, "We can't keep our son from the dangers in this life. We have to prepare him for it. Ultimately it's going to be up to Caleb Burk how he handles his life. I think he will do just fine." Anne slowly nodded her head as she replied, "I know…It's just hard letting go!"

The next morning after saying their goodbyes, Anne and Burk watched Jake and Caleb Burk ride out of sight. Anne did her best. She did not cry until after they left. Burk complained, "Annie girl, you know how much I love you, but dad-burn it, you've got me to bawling!" Anne smiled through her tears as she hugged Burk, "It's alright, Pa. I've never know Jake to fail at anything he sets his mind to…He'll bring back Caleb Burk."

As Jake and Caleb Burk trailed the stolen cattle, Jake said, "We won't have any trouble catching this bunch. The trick is we don't want to catch them too soon. We need to stay far enough behind them to let them get to where they want to go. That way we can stomp every snake in the den. We don't want to get most of them, but leave some stragglers to go back to robbing and killing the next day." Caleb Burk nodded, "I understand, Pa. We will stomp them all."

Jake and Caleb Burk ran a cold camp, no fires. Jake knew how to make himself invisible. He wanted to teach his son the same skills Red Elk taught to him. A common saying among the pioneers was you never knew a Comanche was anywhere around until he tied your hair to his lance.

Jake used an old Comanche trick of trailing an adversary while on a parallel path. When the hunted checked their backtrail, they didn't see anyone. Comanche prided themselves on being a surprise.

Jake and Caleb cautiously watched the exchange of the stolen cattle for money. Antonio was the leader of the Comancheros. He invited Chico, "Why don't you and your men stay with us for a couple of days? We have whiskey to drink and women to use!" Chico sensed that staying would be a fatal mistake. He thought Antonio would like to get his money back by killing him and his men while they slept. Chico replied, "That is a wonderful offer, my good friend! Unfortunately I have other business that must be taken care of. Maybe we can fiesta on our next trip!"

As they watched the bandito gang depart, Jake whispered to Caleb Burk, "We will let the rustlers have a half a day head start. Then we will bring these Comancheros to justice. Afterwards, we will deal with the rustlers." Caleb Burk nodded as he remembered something that Jake had told him, "A Comanche has honor, but not in the same way that a white man has honor. A white man will sometimes want to gun fight with both men getting a chance to draw their guns. A Comanche's honor is satisfied with a dead enemy using whatever means is necessary."

Jake used hand signs to direct Caleb Burk to the opposite side of the Comanchero camp. Jake whispered to his son, "Don't open fire until I shoot first." Jake waited until most of the eight Comancheros were in a drunken stupor. The flickering campfire provided enough shooting light for a Comanche. Jake triggered the first shot. Bullets swarmed like angry bees. Most of the outlaws never got out of their bedrolls, before being stung by .45 slugs. Since the Comancheros were caught in a crossfire, most were struck several times.

As Jake reloaded his Colt, he studied the camp for any movement. When there was none, he shouted to Caleb Burk, "Hold your ground until I say to come down." After toeing all the bodies, the only ones left alive were two frightened women. Jake told them, "Take horses and whatever money you can find on this scum and go home." One woman asked, "You're not going to use us or kill us?" Jake smiled, "You're free to go."

Jake told Caleb Burk, "You did a good job, son." Caleb Burk replied, "Thanks, Pa. Should we bury the bodies?" Jake responded, "Burial is a sign of respect. These men were killers, thieves and cowards. They don't deserve to be buried. Maybe the coyotes and buzzards will get some use out of them." Caleb Burk nodded in agreement. Jake said, "Our job is only half done. We need to finish it with justice to the rustlers. They killed Four/Sixes men. They have to pay."

When Jake had tracked the outlaws to Rosa's cantina, he told Caleb, "We're going to have to play this one a little different. I doubt we can catch these rats all outside that dung hole. I don't want to kill part of them and try to flush the rest out. That would take more time than I want to spend on this scum. Besides, knowing your Ma she's already figuring we're overdue. They don't realize we are after them. I think we can surprise them. I will go in first. You follow right behind me. Use your own judgement on what to do next. I trust your decisions, son."

Jake stepped into the cantina. He quickly moved to the left. Caleb Burk went to the right. Chico couldn't believe his eyes, "Two gringos in my cantina? You must be loco!" Jake smiled, "You the leader of this group of dog turds?" Jake drew his Colt. He put a bullet in Chico. It went through an

26

eye and blasted out the back of Chico's skull. Blood, shards of bone and brain matter splattered the wall of the cantina. Jake fanned his pistol. Each slug ended the life of a bandito.

Jake heard the shots from Caleb Burk's pistol. Jake saw an outlaw slump in death with every shot. In just a few minutes all the renegades were dead or dying. Jake didn't take his eyes off the banditos. He muttered, "That was good shooting, son. I think we got them all."

When the shooting started, Rosa dove for cover behind the bar. Caleb Burk saw a movement out of the corner of his eye. Rosa was crawling around the end of the bar. She pointed the shotgun she was carrying at Jake. The blast caused Jake to wheel towards the sound in a crouch. Caleb had ended Rosa's murderous intent with a bullet between her ample breasts.

Jake stood up and grinned, "Boy, I'm supposed to be taking care of you not the other way around." Caleb Burk joked, "I couldn't let her shoot you. You're the only Pa I got...Besides Ma wouldn't let me hear the end of it." It occurred to Jake that laughing and joking in the face of death was very much the Comanche way.

Anne whooped with joy when she was the two riders, "It's them! It's Jake and Caleb Burk!" Initially they were just two dots on the horizon. Anne's instincts told her who they were. Anne didn't wait for them to dismount. She pulled Caleb Burk out of the saddle, hugging him and showering her son with kisses.

Jake grinned as he looked at Burk, "I'm home too." Burk replied, "You're yesterday's news, boy...And by the way, what took you so long? I'm trying to run a ranch here!" Jake laughed, "It's good to see you too, Burk."

After they had been home for a week, Caleb Burk asked Jake, "Pa, do you think I'll ever have a horse as good as Buck? Jake replied, "A horse like Buck is usually never for sale. Men buy and sell horses all the time, but those horses are not like Buck." Jake could see the frown on his son's face. Jake continued, "Comanche boys caught and trained their own horses. There are still some wild herds in Texas. Maybe you could follow the Comanche way."

Anne threw up her hands in frustration, "Dear God! Caleb Burk, you are bound and determined to put your Ma in an early grave. Surviving those rustlers wasn't enough. Now you want to go chase wild horses?" Anne turned to Jake, "I guess you don't know where your son got this idea?" Jake shrugged but judiciously remained silent. Anne asked, "Did Comanche women ever kill the Comanche men?"

The colt was born in western Texas between the Rio Grande River and Palo Duro Canyon. His lineage could be traced back to the Spanish horses brought to Mexico by the Spanish Conquistadors. The Conquistadors were driven by their search for El Dorado, the mythical city of gold. The Conquistadors were second to none in cruelty and ruthlessness, wiping out entire populations of native people.

Within an hour of his foaling, the colt was on his feet taking wobbly steps as he staggered after his mother. The herd stallion was always proud of new offspring. Within two days the colt's coordination was such that he could gallop fast enough to stay up with the herd.

The predators for wild horses were mountain lions, wolves and the occasional grizzly bear.

When the colt was two months old, he and his mother strayed a little too far from the herd and the protection of the stallion. The bear had been watching them, looking for his opportunity to kill and eat the foal. He started his charge, grunting and snapping his teeth.

The mare was in a panic showing the whites of her eyes, but that didn't stop her from putting herself between her baby and the ferocious grizzly. The mare wheeled and mule-kicked the bear. The kick didn't even slow down the bear bent on getting his next meal.

His charge bowled the mare over and the bear immediately began tearing chunks from her body with his teeth and claws. The mare screamed, but she was out of the earshot of the stallion. The colt could do nothing but cower and watch the bear devour his mother.

The colt was torn between wanting to stay with his mother and survival. The will to live prevailed. He galloped back to the herd. For several days the colt searched the mares looking for his mother. Finally, the laws of nature dictated that it was time to move on.

As a yearling the colt had grown tall, strong and heavily muscled. His father was a dark bay. His mother had been a paint. The colt was a cross between the two, a bay with paint features. The young horse was what the Great Spirit had in mind when he created the horse.

Approaching his second year, the colt had become one of the fastest horses in the herd, second only to the stallion himself. Sometimes the youngster would run just for the sheer joy of running. He also enjoyed out-distancing the other horses who tried to stay up with him. When he had gotten a sufficient distance ahead, the colt would turn on the ones trailing, rear up on his hind legs, whinnying and shaking his head. The message was clear. You cannot outrun me!

In the spring of his second year, the colt's world came apart. The stallion rushed him, nipping and kicking him. The colt was confused. He had always acknowledged that his father was the boss and given the stallion the respect he demanded. Now it seems that his father could no longer tolerate the young horse's presence.

The colt didn't understand that he had become old enough that the stallion viewed him as a rival to be the herd sire. Nature insisted that the good of the species required only the strongest mate. In the horse world the strongest ruled his harem of mares until another stallion proved himself superior through battle. The colt's father had many bite and kick scars to prove he deserved his place in the herd.

The grief stricken young horse was driven from the herd by his father. The bewildered colt tried to rejoin the herd several times, but the fierceness of the stallion's attacks repelled him each time.

Caleb Burk had followed and observed this particular horse herd for several weeks pausing only long enough to hunt and eat. He witnessed the drama of the colt being exiled. Caleb Burk was fascinated by the young horse. He discontinued following the main herd. Instead Caleb Burk chose to trail the colt.

A horse's two greatest impulses are fight or flight. Without the eyes of the other horses, the colt became wary of anything and everything. He had a greater trust in his ability to run from danger then to outfight danger.

The colt began frequenting a small spring-fed creek. Caleb Burk decided to attempt to tame him there. The first encounter consisted of Caleb Burk showing himself at about 50 yards. As soon as the colt saw and smelled the man, he tossed his head, snorted and bolted away at a full gallop.

Caleb Burk didn't want to put too much pressure on the horse at the spring. He remembered the lessons Jake taught him on gentling a young horse. The creek was the one place that he could count on seeing the horse on a regular basis. In the beginning Caleb Burk only came in contact with the horse every third day.

With each new contact the colt took more and more time in assessing the danger that was the man. Finally they had progressed to the point that the colt began looking for Caleb Burk when the horse came for water. Caleb Burk began speaking softly to him, "Aren't you the big one. I've never seen a better looking colt than you. I will call you, Colt."

Caleb Burk started extending a handful of grass at each session. Colt began to notice. The man now spoke to the horse every day in a quiet even tone, "How are you today, Colt? See the tender young grass I brought for you."

The bond between Caleb Burk and Colt continued to grow. Caleb Burk did his best to begin thinking like a horse. Jake had told him that was important to develop a horse that was devoted to his rider. In a herd of horses there is always a pecking order. Position within the herd is largely determined by who can make the other move their feet. Dominance between horses is established by threats of biting and kicking or if needed, actual biting and kicking.

A physical show of power was not needed between this man and this horse. As the trust of Colt for Caleb Burk grew, Colt chose to take the submissive role. The horse eventually allowed Caleb Burk to mount and ride him. Caleb Burk would use the pressure of his legs to let Colt know if he wanted to go slower or faster and in which direction.

Caleb Burk didn't use the constraints of a bridle. It wasn't necessary. Because he allowed the horse complete freedom, the trust between them was the overwhelming factor in their relationship. Caleb Burk knew how much Colt loved to run. He encouraged that. It was exhilarating to fly across the prairie on Colt's back. The man loved it as much as the horse.

Caleb Burk made camp for the night by starting a small fire to cook whatever meat he had, either deer, antelope or rabbit. When he was finished, Caleb Burk moved his camp a couple of miles from where he ate before bedding down. That reduced the chances of a predator or unfriendly Indians from finding him. He always made sure he slept next to good forage for Colt.

One night Caleb Burk was awakened by a snort from Colt. He could make out a dozen dark shapes sneaking around his camp. It was a pack of red wolves. The wolf pack was slowly closing their circle around Caleb Burk and Colt.

The first wolf launched himself at Caleb Burk. The second jumped on Colt's back, biting the back of his neck. The first wolf was met in midair by a bullet from Caleb Burk's sixshooter. The blast didn't seem to register on the rest of the wolves.

The other wolves were looking for an opening to join the attack on the man and the horse. The wolves' ribs were showing as their hunting had not produced enough meat to go around. They were hungry!

Colt was bucking, kicking and screaming, but not in fear. Instead it was in anger. He jumped so high that when all four feet hit the ground, it catapulted the wolf off of his back. Caleb Burk dispatched that wolf with a .45 slug from his gun.

The wolves were ravenous. They were desperate to eat. The gunshots had not discouraged them. Caleb Burk snapped off another shot at a dark form. The yip from the wolf announced the arrival of the bullet.

Instead of running away which would have been the response of most horses, Colt bit, struck with his forelegs and kicked every wolf he could see. One by one the wolves were killed or slinked off with injuries. The final tally showed six dead wolves. Six more had retreated to lick their wounds.

At daylight Caleb Burk found the plant that Jake had shown him to apply to injured flesh. He lovingly treated Colt's wound.

Colt had become noticeably restless. After giving him his head when on their daily ride, Colt showed Caleb Burk the source of his restlessness. It was the herd. When Colt whinnied to them, Caleb Burk slid from his back. He wanted the horse to have the total freedom to do his own will.

At Colt's whinny, his father reared up on his hind legs prancing. The stallion blasted a scream of warning to the young horse before charging him.

Colt no longer considered the stallion as his father. His genetic makeup didn't allow it. To Colt, the stallion was just another horse. One who Colt was going to challenge for the position of herd master and sire.

Colt galloped to meet the big stud. Colt was angry and defiant. He was eager for battle. Both horses went to their knees as their necks snaked back and forth trying to deliver a crippling bite to the other's legs. The stallion's vast experience gave him the advantage. Soon blood was flowing from Colt's legs. Fortunately, the wounds were superficial and not crippling.

Colt's youthful stamina kicked in as he sprang to his feet kicking and biting the old horse. Even though he had sent many challengers away in defeat, the stallion began to realize that he wasn't going to win this fight.

After being beaten down and injured, the old herd sire galloped away trying to escape with his life. Colt chased him for a short time before whinnying a warning for him not to return. The old stallion suffered the same fate as all herd sires eventually succumb to. He would live out the balance of his life in exile.

Colt turned his attention to showing dominance to his new herd of mares. They all meekly deferred to him. Caleb Burk smiled at the crowning of the new herd boss. He knew that his relationship with Colt was forever changed.

Caleb Burk returned to the box canyon where he had left the ranch pony. He had put up a barrier to keep the horse inside the canyon. There was plenty of green grass and a small spring-fed pool of water. As he saddled the horse, Caleb Burk couldn't help feeling a twinge of sadness at the loss of Colt. He had been gone from the ranch for a month. Caleb Burk knew his Pa would eventually come looking for him sooner or later. He smiled at the thought of his Ma daily demanding that Jake go bring their boy back.

Caleb Burk pointed the nose of his horse towards the Four-Sixes. It was time to go home. That afternoon Caleb Burk was startled to hear a familiar nicker. He twisted in his saddle to see Colt come trotting up. As Colt nuzzled him, Caleb Burk wondered, "What is it? I don't understand. You were the herd boss. Why are you here?" Caleb Burk hopped over to the broad back of Colt. Colt continued in the direction that his rider wanted. Caleb Burk laughed out loud with the realization that Colt had chosen him over the herd.

Jake was helping the hands work cattle in a west pasture. He saw the two horses before the others did. The lone rider sat on his horse that could only be Caleb Burk. Jake crossed a leg over his saddle horn waiting for his son. As Caleb Burk got closer, he called out, "Howdy, Pa! It's good to see you!"

The rest of the cowboys' jaws dropped. Caleb was riding a beautiful mustang without a saddle or bridle. A ranch pony with its reins knotted over his neck dutifully trotted behind the mustang. Jake responded as he stroked his chin, "That's a mighty fine animal you're riding. It looks like y'all may be friends."

After hearing Caleb Burk tell Colt's complete story, the cowhands shook their heads in amazement. Sandy Young gave a low whistle, "If I wasn't looking at it with my own eyes, I'd never believed it!" Jake stated, "No Comanche could have done better than what you've done, son. I am sure proud of you. Go on to the house or your Ma will have a conniption fit if she finds you dawdled with us." Father and son enjoyed a laugh together.

Little Earl was born as William Earl Johnson to cotton farmers, Earl and Jolene Johnson. Early in life he was called Little Earl. His father was Big Earl. The Johnson's barely eked out a living by raising cotton and a few pigs on their hard-scrabble 40 acres in southwestern Oklahoma.

Earl and Jolene first noticed something was different about their baby when he seemed indifferent to their hugs and kisses. Sometimes he tolerated it, but most of the time, he turned away from them.

By the time he was three, Earl and Jolene had lost any semblance of control of Little Earl. If he wanted something, he threw a tantrum. It was not like a normal baby's tantrum. No amount of attention or even a couple of good, healthy whacks on his bottom could deter Little Earl. Finally his parents gave up. It was much easier to give Little Earl what he wanted. At least they could enjoy a little peace once in a while even if it was short lived.

Little Earl hated his parents. They represented authority to him. He could not tolerate someone trying to tell him what to do.

The summer of Little Earl's eighth year, Big Earl had enough. At dawn he told Little Earl, "I want you to help me plow today." Little Earl responded with contempt, "Why would I want to do that. Do you think I want to grow up and be some stupid farmer like you?"

Big Earl grabbed the boy's shoulders and shook him, "That's it. I've put up with this all I'm going to. Starting today there's going to be some big changes around here!" Little Earl grinned, "Sure, Pa, whatever you say." Big Earl was speechless.

Big Earl had traded a hog for an old Colt .45. It was his only means of defending his family. He kept it loaded as there were still a few hostile Indians around. If the Cheyenne came, Big Earl wanted to be ready. Little Earl retrieved the old gun from its hiding place. He cocked the gun and said to his father, "You're right, Pa. It's time there were some changes around here."

Little Earl pulled the trigger. The bullet punctured Big Earl's heart. He was dead when he hit the dirt floor of the old shack. Little Earl thought, "That was a pretty good shot. I bet I could get really good with this gun with a little practice."

Jolene heard the gunshot while outside hanging clothes to dry. She ran inside fearing the worst. Jolene cradled Big Earl's head in her lap as she cried, "Little Earl, what happened? Did you do this? Was it an accident?" The uninterested expression never changed on Little Earl's face. "No, Ma. It was no accident. Pa said there needed to some changes around here. He was right."

Jolene looked down the barrel of the Colt that Little Earl was aiming at her, in horror. She managed to blurt out, "God, no!" before Little Earl fired the gun. He watched in satisfaction as his mother died at his feet.

Little Earl packed up and loaded everything of value on the old mule. He stuck the .45 in his rope belt, mounted the mule and rode off without a backward glance. Little Earl never thought about his parents again for the rest of his life.

He had ridden about 10 miles when he was surrounded by a small Cheyenne war party. The Indians were intrigued by this farm boy. Despite their war cries and threatening gestures with their tomahawks, Little Earl never flinched.

One of the Cheyenne dragged the boy off the mule and pressed a knife to his throat. Blood started to trickle from the sharp edge of the blade. Little Earl remained expressionless.

Viho lifted his hand, "Stop! My wife and I have no children. I like his courage. I will take him to my teepee to Jaya. We will raise him as our own. He will grow straight and tall. I will call him, Little Wolf. He will make me proud."

As many would find out down through the years, it was not courage that Viho saw. It was a lack of emotion.

Jaya was standing at the entrance to their teepee to welcome Viho home. Her forehead furrowed when she saw the small, white boy riding behind Viho. Viho smiled, "Wife, meet your new son, Little Wolf." Jaya was overjoyed. She had been living with the stigma of being childless. Jaya would no longer have to tuck her head when around the other mothers.

Little Wolf revealed an insight into who he was when he was pushed down by a Cheyenne boy twice his size. Little Wolf attacked the larger youth with such ferocity that he had him pinned on his back furiously pummeling him. It took two of the Cheyenne women to pull him off. They were afraid the bigger boy was going to be killed.

Word of the one-sided fight quickly spread throughout the village. Viho swelled with pride when he heard of Little Wolf's victory. His son was going to be a great warrior. Viho knew nothing about the saying, "Sow the wind, reap the whirlwind."

Over the next two years, Little Wolf established a reputation as being fearless. He was also known for being merciless. One day it occurred to Little Wolf that it was time for another change. He was weary of the older Indians telling him what to do. He needed to go somewhere where people minded their own business.

Even though Viho and Jaya had treated him like their own son, he was sick of them most of all. That night in his last act as Little Wolf, he slit their throats then stole two horses from the remuda. He rode for two days straight, switching horses when one needed a rest.

Some of the Cheyenne tracked him for a week. They finally gave up and returned to the village when they determined they weren't getting any closer. The leader said, "I think we are tracking a demon. You cannot kill a demon." Little Wolf's name lived in infamy among the Cheyenne to describe lack of loyalty and treachery.

Little Earl had brought his bow and arrows. He managed to keep himself fed by killing rabbits and birds. He also had stolen back his old Colt .45.

Little Earl sat on a rise observing the Bar S cattle ranch. He rode down the hill into the camp. The foreman pushed his hat back on his head and asked, "Boy, where'd you get them Indian ponies?" Little Earl retorted, "What business is it of yours?" The foreman thought for a minute before laughing, "Well, ain't you just the little curly wolf? Do you have a name?" Little Earl said, "Of course I got a name... It's Little Earl."

The foreman continued, "Well...Little Earl, you look like you could use a good meal. You looking for work?" Little Earl was tired of his rabbit and songbird diet. He lied, "I ain't real hungry, but I guess I could eat some." The foreman said, "Ol' Cookie over there will rustle you up some grub. Come see me afterwards and we'll talk about you working for the Bar S. By the way, I got me a name too. It's Wendell."

Wendell felt sorry for the young boy. He outfitted Little Earl with clothes including a hat and boots. He even cut down a worn holster so Little Earl could carry his Colt. Wendell took a personal interest in teaching Little Earl how to herd cattle.

His two years with the Cheyenne had made Little Earl an excellent rider. The rest of the cowboys admired that. This group of cowhands didn't talk much. Little Earl fit right in.

Every night after supper, Little Earl practiced drawing his .45. In a few months he became lightning quick in grabbing the butt of his gun and clearing his holster. Wendell had given him a half a box of cartridges for his Colt. Whenever he could distance himself where he was far enough away from the herd so as not to spook the cattle, Little Earl would practice using tree limbs or cactus as targets.

Little Earl used every penny of his pay to buy .45 shells. He was obsessed with his Colt. Little Earl couldn't get enough of drawing and firing his pistol. He was always polishing it with an old rag.

When he turned 14, Little Earl decided it was time for yet another change. The old foreman had long recognized that Little Earl did better when he asked him to do something instead of telling him.

Today, Wendell was in a hurry and didn't feel like observing the nicesities, "Little Earl, you're gonna be helping with branding today." Little Earl responded, "I will if I feel like it." Wendell was exasperated, "Looky here, you young whelp. Just do what I tell you without all the sass."

The slug from Little Earl's Colt blew half of Wendell's head off. The rest of the cowboys were stunned. Little Earl still had his smoking gun drawn. He quickly checked the eyes of each one. There were no challengers.

Little Earl calmly filled his saddle bags with food, tied a bedroll to the back of his saddle and loped off. The cold look in his eyes along with the speed and accuracy of his gunplay, discouraged anyone from following him. The cowboys at the Bar S had talked about what a great town Fort Worth was. Little Earl pointed the nose of his horse south.

A covered wagon was lurching in his direction. As it got closer, Little Earl could see the smiling faces of a young married couple. The man called out to him, "It's a beautiful day today. Don't you agree, brother?" Little Earl put bullets in the center of their chests. Before the man's eyes closed in death, he croaked, "Why?" Little Earl answered, "I ain't your brother."

Little Earl looted their wagon finding the cash that was their nest egg. He laughed as he counted it, "I don't need no damn job. There will always be sheep like these two ready to be sheared."

Decatur was a little town just north of Fort Worth. Little Earl was tired of riding. He took a break by tying his horse at the hitching rail and stepping up on the wooden sidewalk. Little Earl was heading for the saloon when he accidently bumped into a cowboy.

The cowboy was in town from a Wise County ranch. He had just been paid and was already half drunk. Little Earl spit, "Watch where you're going, son of a bitch." The cowboy grinned as he responded, "Easy, kid. I meant no harm." Little Earl's hand went to the butt of his gun, "I ain't no kid."

The cowboy looked at his buddy, "What do you think, pard? Should I turn this little punk over my knee for a good, old fashioned whipping like my Pa always done to me when

I needed it?" His buddy shrugged his shoulders. At first the cowboy didn't take Little Earl seriously. The situation turned deadly.

Little Earl kept pushing, "Well, what's it going to be shit kicker? I'm ready for my whupping." The cowboy angrily went for his gun. He didn't even clear his holster before the force of the .45 slug blasted him off the sidewalk into the street.

When the sheriff came to investigate, some of the witnesses said that the kid was so fast they never saw him draw. It seemed like the gun jumped into his hand. All agreed that the cowboy went for his gun first. It was self-defense.

The grizzled sheriff spoke to Little Earl, "Well, I guess I don't have anything to hold you on, but I want you to get on your horse and ride until you're out of Decatur." Little Earl snorted defiantly, "I ain't done nothing wrong and I'm not going anywhere till I have me a drink!"

Little Earl squared off against the lawman. The sheriff was uneasy for two reasons. One was the reports of how fast this boy was on the draw. The second was the look in Little Earl's eyes. It was that blank, soulless look that the sheriff once saw in the eyes of an angry rattlesnake.

The sheriff sputtered, "Well,,,I guess that will be okay, but one drink and I want you gone." Little Earl sneered, "Are you asking or telling?" The sheriff said meekly, "Seeing as how you ain't broke no law, I guess I'm asking."

Little Earl didn't give him the courtesy of an answer. He swiveled on his heels and headed for the saloon. Little Earl had developed a thirst for whiskey at the Bar S when he stole from the cowboy's bottles whenever Wendell wasn't looking.

Little Earl was prepared to pay for his whisky as he was flush with blood-stained cash. He never got the chance. The local riffraff kept his glass full, all the while congratulating him on being the fastest gun in Texas and backing down the Decatur sheriff. Little Earl discovered an emotion that day that he more than liked. He loved to see fear ooze out of the pores of another human being.

Little Earl made a name for himself in Fort Worth. He padded his reputation with a string of killings of down-on-their-luck cowboys, peddlers and shop keepers. Little Earl became the man to see to do someone else's dirty work. If you wanted someone dead and you had the money, Little Earl took care of it. The age and gender of his victims were of no consequence.

A few of the local thieves invited him into their schemes of robbery, thinking he would provide good protection. The problem with their plans were in the dividing of the loot. Little Earl paid in lead. After a number of the outlaws were found with their bodies riddled with bullet holes, the pool of potential partners dried up.

Stacy Green was a respected banker. His gambling habit got out of control leaving his personal financial situation with a substantial deficit. It was large enough to put his holdings in the bank in jeopardy.

He held a clandestine meeting with Little Earl in the back of a livery stable the bank owned. Green explained what needed to be done. "Mr. Johnson, I need you to rob my bank. Whatever you steal is covered by insurance. We will split the cash. You may keep half for your trouble."

Little Earl laughed, "That sounds good, Mr. Green. You got a deal." Little Earl had laughed inwardly at the notion that he would split the money. He knew he wouldn't do that.

Little Earl successfully robbed the bank thanks to a door that was conveniently left unlocked. Green was deliriously happy. The bank lost $100,000. That meant his half of the cash would bail him out of his predicament. When summoned to a meeting to give Green his share, Little Earl laughed in the messenger's face. "Tell Mr. Green to be happy I'm gonna let him live. That's all he's getting from me."

It seems that there is always some low-life who will do anything for money. Green met with one and offered him $500 to kill Little Earl. The thing that Little Earl loved the most was that others feared him. The assassin was scared, but he wanted that money.

That night Little Earl stepped out of the saloon to stretch his legs. He was silhouetted by the light from the bar. The assassin shakily aimed the iron sights of the Winchester 30-30 to the middle of Little Earl's chest. The shot caromed off the overhead saloon sign.

Little Earl fanned his sixgun in the direction of the muzzle flash. He quickly reloaded. After a sustained period of silence, Little Earl checked the alley where the assassin attempted his drygulch. The man was dead.

Josephine was carrying her little girl to the doctor's office. Beth had the croup that was getting worse by the hour. Josephine decided not to wait till morning to take her to Doc Smith. The kindly old doctor had always told Josephine that he was available if she needed him any hour of the day or night.

Little Earl heard the footsteps on the wooden sidewalk behind him. He turned and fired blindly. Josephine felt the bullet slam into Beth. She lay the child down to examine her. Josephine screamed, "Beth has been shot! She's dead!" When Little Earl stepped out of the darkness with his gun drawn, he sneered, "You must be some kind of bad momma to have your kid out at this hour. This kind of thing is what happens when a kid is someplace they ain't supposed to be!"

Josephine doubled up her fists and charged Little Earl as she screamed, "I'm going to kill you!" He shot her in the belly. As she moaned and squirmed on the sidewalk, Little Earl shot her a second time. He announced, "And that's what happens to anybody who threatens me, damn woman or not!"

Later when Little Earl made a call on Stacy Green to even up the score of hiring someone to kill him, he discovered that Green was nowhere to be found. Green left town at a gallop and was never heard from again. He abandoned his wife of ten years and four small children.

When Jake and Caleb Burk came in from working cows, Anne was crying into a crumpled up handkerchief. Jake asked, "What's happened, honey?" Anne stopped sobbing long enough to whisper, "I got word today from our neighbor, Mrs. Higgins that my old childhood friend, Josephine Sanders and her baby have been murdered. Shot down in the streets of Ft. Worth...It's just so awful." Jake responded, "What about the law? They have a sheriff in Ft. Worth." Anne frowned, "Mrs. Wiggins didn't say why. She just said the law wasn't doing anything about it."

Jake furrowed his brow, "How did Mrs. Higgins know you were Josephine's old friend?" Anne replied, "She didn't. I realized who it was when she told me Josephine's name."

Jake continued, "Still, even though she's our neighbor, Mrs. Wiggins came a ways to bring you this news." Anne nodded, "I think she really wanted you to know about it. Some folks around here think you are some kind of avenging angel. It seems you are a hero to them."

Jake grinned, "A hero and an angel?" Anne rolled her eyes, "I can give you the hero part. You're my hero...but if they knew you better, they would know you're no angel!" Caleb Burk had listened to everything that was said. Jake asked as Caleb Burk started looking his Pa up and down, "Son, what are you doing?" Caleb Burk continued examining Jake, "Nothing much, Pa. just trying to see if you've sprouted wings." Jake took a playful, back-handed swing at his son that Caleb Burk easily dodged.

After supper Jake announced, "I reckon I'll take a ride over to Ft. Worth in the morning to see if a woman and her child were murdered or if there's more to it than that." Caleb Burk asked, "Can I go with you, Pa?" Jake saw the disappointment on his face when Jake replied, "No, son. I need you to tend to things around here." Burk Burnett interjected, "Good, cause I got a ranch to run!" Later when they were alone, Jake explained, "Your Ma isn't doing well over the death of her friend. I want you to look after her. I need to know she's going to be alright." Caleb Burk nodded, "I understand. I'll see after her, Pa."

Jake shook hands with Sheriff Nick Wale. Jake accepted the Sheriff's offer to have a seat. Jake turned a little less cordial, "Sheriff, there's a rumor that a woman and child were murdered in Ft. Worth. Can you shed some light on what happened?" Sheriff Wale responded, "First, let me say it's good to see you again. Jake, this case sticks in my craw like no other. The little girl was shot by accident from a stray bullet. One of the local low-lifes was trying to kill Little Earl Johnson…I will say this. If there was a man who needs killing, it's Johnson. Little Earl killed who I'm sure was a paid assassin."

Wale paused to offer Jake a cup of coffee. Jake shook his head, "I would rather hear the rest of this story." The Sheriff took a quick sip from his cup, "After Little Earl killed the man who was after him, Little Earl said he heard someone behind him. He claimed he thought it was another gunman coming for him. That's when the child was shot. When Josephine saw her daughter was dead, she went after Little Earl. Witnesses said she wasn't armed, but Little Earl shot her anyway…Dammit all to hell, the sum bitch didn't have to shoot her. He even put a second round in her!"

Jake pushed his hat back on his head, "Wale, you mean to tell me that you can't do nothing about this?" Sheriff Wale sighed, "If Josephine hadn't threatened to kill Little Earl, he'd be in a cell right now. As it is, my hands are tied. I swore to follow the law. There's nothing I can legally do!"

Jake's eyes narrowed, "The only swearing I ever done was to an old Comanche. I swore I would make things right if I could." As Jake strode out of the sheriff's office, the Sheriff said softly, "Happy hunting, my friend."

Jake located Little Earl in the White Elephant Saloon. He listened quietly as Little Earl bragged to his audience, "I reckon I'm the fastest gun that ever was! My hands are so quick most folks can't see them move. I ain't never been beat on the draw. Thems that tried are all dead!"

One of the onlookers asked, "Who gave you the most trouble, Little Earl? With as many men as you done kilt, there had to be one that came close to out-drawing you."

Little Earl grinned, "Well maybe there…" Little Earl was interrupted by Jake, "Yeah, tell us gunslinger. Who gave you the most problem? Was it that unarmed young momma who you gunned down? I bet she scared the shit out of you…or maybe it was her little baby girl that you shot? Shooting babies can really test a man's nerve."

Little Earl rose from the table, "Who the hell are you, mister? I need to know what to tell the undertaker to put on your marker! You obviously ain't figured out who I am. I am Little Earl Johnson, the fastest gun there ever was!"

Jake eyes became slits as he squared up against Little Earl, "My name is Jake Jackson." There was a collective gasp from the bar patrons. Someone whispered, "It is him. I seen him before!" Little Earl sneered, "I don't give a damn who you are! Your party's about to be over!" Jake smiled, "There's one thing I can't make up my mind about." Little Earl snorted, "And what would that be?" Jake replied, "I can't rightly decide if I should scalp you are not."

An enraged Little Earl went for his gun. Little Earl was fast. He got most of his gun out of the holster before being thumped in the chest by Jake's first bullet. Jake continued to fan his pistol until it was empty. When he was finished, you could cover all six holes with a playing card.

No one in the bar was expecting that type of gunplay. The type of gunplay that had never been seen before. The type of gunplay that was unlikely to ever be seen again. While the crowd was confused trying to get past their amazement, Jake stooped over the body and made one quick slash with his skinning knife. Jake threw the bloody scalp on the bar. The owners of the saloon nailed the scalp over the bar as testimony that the great Jake Jackson had indeed been there.

Back at the Four-Sixes Jake hugged and kissed his wife. He spoke softly, "The man who murdered your friend and her baby, won't be killing anybody else."

Jake had made many memories in his life. Some he shared with Anne. Some he did not. Tonight Jake was feeling the cool breezes as he relaxed on the porch. He closed his eyes as his mind drifted back to a memory that was before he met Anne.

Jake sighed deeply. When he was younger, it didn't take much to push him into a fight. These days he had seen so much killing that he was sick of it. It was always some young whelp like this bellowing kid trying to make a name for himself by taking down the legendary Jake Jackson.

Jake turned to face the boy. There was a world of difference between the two. Jake had a weathered face that he had earned from a lifetime spent outdoors usually on the back of a horse. The young upstart had the smooth, unwrinkled face of a baby. His skin was pale from spending his time in dark saloons.

Jake's clothes were as worn as his face. His hat, shirt, jeans and jacket were practical and fit him like a second skin. The kid had a shiny black leather vest with silver conchos. His brand new hat set at a jaunty angle on his head. Everything about the kid's outfit said "Look at me!"

The Colt 45 in Jake's holster was plain with most of the bluing rubbed off from the countless times Jake had drawn his gun, in practice and in self-defense. Its wooden handle fit Jake's hand perfectly also from being well used.

The boy's sixshooter was silver plated with a pearl handle. Everything about his gun shined. He didn't practice much because he was naturally fast. The boy thought that was all it took. He spent more time polishing his pistol than practicing with it.

The kid smirked, "Hey, old man! I ain't gonna say it again! Your time is come and gone. Every herd bull gets replaced by one younger and stronger. I don't want to have to kill you... I tell you what. If you get down on your hands and knees, I'll let you crawl out of here."

The kid glanced at his whiskey buddies to see if they thought that was as funny as he did. They were guffawing and slapping each other on the back over the antics of their new hero. The group was a bunch of saddle tramps and cutthroats. They had seen the kid practice draw. It was like lightning. They swore no one could be as fast as the kid.

Jake said in an even voice, "Son, you best..." The kid interrupted, "Shut up, grandpa! I ain't your damn son! I knowed you might have been something a long time ago, but not no more!" The bartender whispered to the kid, "Don't you know who that is? That's Jake Jackson." The kid replied, "You can shut up too or you'll be next!"

The kid continued, "Just so you'll know who plugged you, I'm the Oklahoma Kid. I cut my teeth on you Texas jaspers. Take a look at them notches on my gun. You probably can't count that high!" That prompted another round of laughter from the kid's followers.

The truth was the kid had only killed two men. Only one of them was a face to face gunfight. That was against a farm boy wearing a cap and ball pistol stuck in the rope holding his pants up. The kid goaded him by saying, "Phew! Something smells like chicken shit! I think that's you sodbuster!" When the farm boy drew, the barrel of his gun snagged on the rope. The kid shot him anyway.

The second was when the kid was showing off by twirling his gun. It went off accidently killing an innocent bystander. The kid exclaimed, "Did y'all see that. That sidewinder was fixin' to shoot me!" Most knew that the town dentist didn't even carry a gun. The kid counted that as a gun fight.

The kid continued, "Well, what's it gonna be old timer, crawl or draw?"

Jake briefly considered trying to wing him in the shoulder, but discarded that as being too risky. You never know how fast some of these young punks really are. And besides, anybody can get lucky. Jake hadn't lived this long by being careless. He tried one more time, "Okay kid, there ain't no reason for you to die here today. Why don't you back off. I'll buy you a beer and we'll call it a day."

The kid's face turned rooster red in anger. He spat out his words, "Oh, someone is gonna die here today, but it won't be me!...You're out of time!" Both men went for their guns. The kid was fast, real fast. Both guns barked as one. The gun smoke from both barrels swirled upward, joining the cigarette and cigar smoke that choked the saloon.

The bullet from the kid's gun whizzed by Jake's head barely nicking his earlobe. Meanwhile, Jake's slug went in the kid's head exactly between his eyes. When it exited, it left a huge hole in the back of the kid's skull as blood and brain matter oozed out mixing in with the tobacco quid on the barroom floor.

The patrons of the saloon collectively held their breath. They were shocked into silence. Jake faced the kid's buddies, "Crawl or draw." The six backslappers hit the floor and scurried out the batwing doors of the bar on all fours.

The bartender addressed Jake, "Gunfighter..." Jake responded, "What?" The bartender grinned, "Thanks for taking out the trash. Your beer is on the house."

The prettiest unmarried girl in town was Polly Gentry. She had long, curly blonde hair. Her mesmerizing eyes were the color of the blue sky at dawn. She had turned down the overtures of every bachelor in town plus a few married ones.

Polly's daddy, George, owned the only bank in town. He tried to send her back east to his sister's hoping Polly would find a husband more suitable to her station in life. Polly told him, "Daddy, I love Aunt Sue, but I'm not going back there to marry some old stuffed shirt. I love life here. I love the open spaces and riding horses. You know that!"

George sputtered, "Polly, you know I've done my best raising you since your mama died, but staying here is not fair to you. There are greater things in this world than our little town." Polly answered, "Daddy, I'm not going! I don't want to hear any more about it." George shrugged his shoulders in resignation with his head-strong daughter.

When Jake passed Polly on the wooden sidewalk, he tipped his hat. Polly batted her eyelashes and gave him a big smile. Jake kept on walking. Polly turned and watched Jake disappear from sight. A small pout was on her lips. She couldn't remember ever being ignored before.

From then on, a good part of Polly's day was spent day dreaming about Jake. She realized he was old enough to be her father, but she didn't care. Polly was fascinated with the gunfighter. He wasn't boring like the other men in town.

She asked George, "Daddy, I'm thinking about asking Mr. Jackson for supper one night. Would that be alright with you?" George looked like he had been hit across the back of his head with an axe handle. Finally, he managed to choke out, "Polly, are you insane? Absolutely, not!"

Polly grinned as she got the reaction she expected. She smiled sweetly and said, "But, Daddy, why not?" George's ears turned bright red as he shouted, "Why not?!! Why not?!! He's an outlaw! He kills people for a living! I don't want him near you! If you see him on the street, you run the other direction!"

Polly continued smiling, "But, Daddy, if he's an outlaw like you say he is then why doesn't the sheriff arrest him?" George sputtered and stammered without answering. "You heard what I said, young lady. I don't want you around Jake Jackson. The man's dangerous!" Polly immediately began plotting how she could get Jake to come to supper.

George hired spies to follow Polly every time she left the house. They all reported the same thing. She was seen trying to engage Jake in conversation, but the gunfighter had done nothing but be polite.

Red Fitzpatrick was aptly named with an unruly shock of red hair. That was not what made him famous. He was known for his trigger temper and the hair-triggers on his twin Colts. Red wore his pistols in a double cross draw holster. Some considered him the fastest gun hand in the west. Red was a killer for hire. He was not cheap, but you went to him when you needed someone dangerous killed. Red had never been beaten.

Red received a telegram from George Gentry. It said that the local bank was holding a $1000 deposit from George to him with a promise of $10,000 more at the completion of the job. The hired assassin gave a low whistle, "This must be someone mighty hard to kill at this price." The next morning

Red saddled his horse and packed provisions. He spurred his black stud into a gallop. Red was in a hurry to meet his $10,000.

The black stud trotted up to the biggest house in town. He was glistening with sweat. Red had ridden him too hard...again. To Red's way of thinking, a horse was only good for transportation. He felt that in his occupation, a man shouldn't have feelings for people much less a horse.

Red strode up to the front door and knocked loudly. A frantic George quickly opened the door and motioned Red inside. Before George shut the door, he nervously checked to make sure no one had seen Red enter his house.

Red asked, "What the hell is wrong with you? I ain't never seen a man as jumpy as you." George took Red by the arm and guided him into the parlor. After shutting the thick oaken doors, George said, "We're going to have to be careful. I have a reputation to think of. I can't let people think I've hired Red Fitzpatrick."

While he nodded his head in agreement, Red made a mental note to blackmail George after the job. He was sure he could squeeze more money from the banker. George explained the situation with his daughter. He wanted Jake Jackson eliminated from Polly's life.

Red grinned, "You want me to kill Jake Jackson... the gunfighter?" George gulped and timidly replied, "Yes." Red rolled his eyes, "Well in that case, I'm gonna have to have more money. Let's say another five grand?" George reluctantly agree, "Okay."

George felt like Red had him over a barrel. He didn't think he had any choice if he wanted Jake dead. What George didn't realize was that Red's barrel was way bigger than what George thought it was. Red would not stop extorting money from George until he had every last cent. Before he left, Red warned George, "Just so we're clear, do you know what will happen to you if you don't pay me my money?" George nodded. He knew.

As Polly fell in beside him when Jake was walking to the hardware store, she blurted out, "Isn't it a beautiful day?" Jake had finally had enough, "Little lady, what kind of game are you playing?"

Polly smiled even brighter, "Oh Mr. Jackson, I can assure you this is no game." Jake retorted, "Okay then, what do you want?" Polly said, "I thought you would never ask. I want you to come to my house for supper." Jake shook his head, "You're just a kid. Don't you know I'm old enough to be your daddy?" Polly boldly replied, "I am not a kid and when I look at you, the last thing I think of is my daddy!" Jake was a little taken aback by the young woman's boldness.

Jake couldn't help, but to think of Macy. Macy was the most beautiful woman he had ever seen. Her jet black hair and soulful eyes coupled with her full ruby red lips always took his breath away. Jake fell in love with her the first time he saw her. They later married. It was easily the happiest time in his life.

That life of bliss ended when Jake came home and found Macy and their baby boy slaughtered by a gang of renegades. Jake hunted down and killed every member of the gang. Most experienced a gruesome and painful demise. Jake was never the same after losing his family.

Jake said to Polly, "I don't think supper is a good idea. I bet your daddy doesn't either. Thanks for the invite, but I'm gonna have to pass." Polly stomped her foot in frustration.

Everyone knew Red Fitzpatrick was in town. He didn't exactly blend in with the red hair. The bartender at the saloon asked Jake, "You have any idea why Red Fitzpatrick is in town?" Jake just shook his head, no. Jake knew Red, but didn't keep track of his comings and goings.

At that moment Red pushed open the swinging doors and stepped into the barroom, all conversation immediately stopped. Everyone's focus was on Red. Red saw Jake and nodded his head, "Jake." Jake nodded back, "Red."

Red motioned to the spot next to Jake at the bar, "Mind if I join you?" Jake replied, "It's a free country." Red drank about half his beer before he spoke again, "I was sorry to hear about Macy." Virgil responded in a flat voice, "Thanks."

After he finished his beer, Red said, "No point in beating around the bush, Jake. I'm here to kill you." Jake's expression never changed. Red continued, "I'll be out in the street tomorrow at high noon. No shame if you cleared out tonight." They both knew there was no chance of that happening. Just before Red left the saloon, he explained, "This visit was a professional courtesy. I'll see you tomorrow."

Jake slept soundly every night. Even though he had killed many men, his conscious was clear. Jake only used his gun in defending himself or those who couldn't defend themselves. The only disruption to his sleep was when he dreamed of Macy. He didn't fear death because he knew Macy was waiting for him on the other side.

Jake awoke to an overcast day that threatened to rain. He was a little taken aback when he went to the café for breakfast. The small town was packed with people. Some had driven in from the surrounding ranches and farms. Word had quickly spread of the impending, epic gunfight. The argument about who was faster, Red or Jake, was about to be settled once and for all.

The crowd voiced their encouragements. "Good luck, Mr. Jackson." "We're pulling for you, Mr. Jackson." It seems no one had anything good to say to Red.

After breakfast Jake decided to bid his time at the saloon until noon. Many offered to buy him a drink which Jake refused with a shake of his head. Finally, the bartender said loudly, "People, Mr. Jackson doesn't want a drink. He has important business to take care of today. Besides, after today his money ain't gonna be any good here. His drinks are free." The bartender wasn't being as generous as some might think. He had never seen Jake drink more than two beers in a day.

Polly was puzzled. Why did this hateful, ugly man come to town to kill her Jake? Suddenly the pieces fell into place. She marched down to the bank and into her daddy's office. Polly shouted, "Daddy, please tell me you don't have anything to do with this gunfight today!" Instead of answering, George just looked down at his desk. Polly's hand went to her mouth as she gasped. "Daddy, how could you? I thought you loved me." George mumbled, "I do love you, dear. That's why I brought Red here."

Polly began to cry. George got up to console her. As he put his hand on her shoulder, Polly flung his hand away, "Don't touch me. Don't ever touch me again."

As noon approached, the tension in the crowd was palatable. People who had not known or even seen Red or Jake became nervous. The waitress dropped a dish in the café. Those eating there jumped. A few swore. The cook exclaimed "Lord girl, would you please be careful? Today ain't the day for that!"

Red pulled on his gloves and stepped out into the street. Someone looking through a window at the saloon said, "Ol' Red is out there." Jake slipped his gun in and out of his holster a couple of times to make sure it wasn't sticking. He took his place facing Red.

Red warned, "Jake, it ain't too late. You can still ride out." Jake replied, "Let's get on with it." Both men pulled their guns and fired. For years afterwards, those who were there and those who claimed they were there, said that it seemed impossible that anyone could draw as fast as the two men.

The gunshots were identical. Red was a fraction of a second faster. His bullet went through Jake's right shoulder. The force of the bullet caused Jake's slug to miss a couple of inches. Red's injury was a flesh wound in his side.

As his gun hand was now disabled, Jake was helpless. He lifted his chin waiting for the killing shot. Red cocked his Colt, "Well goodbye, pard. Tell the devil I'll see him soon."

Polly had been watching from the front porch of the bank. When she saw that Jake was hit, she flew from the porch and dove shielding Jake's body with hers. The bullet from Red's gun struck her in the back.

Red muttered, "Crazy damn girl." The sound of a rifle split the quiet. Red was shoved violently from behind. He looked down in amazement as blood gushed from his chest. Red crumpled to the ground as he began his journey to meet the devil.

The rifle sounded a second time. George had nothing else to live for with Polly dead. The slug went in under his chin and out the top of his head. He was dead instantly.

Jake gently laid Polly down. He detected a slight rising and falling of her chest. He yelled, "Get the doc! Polly is still alive!"

It took several months for Polly to recover. Once she did, she took over the management of the bank. Jake visited her every day. One day, Jake squeezed her hand, "Polly, it's time for me to be moving on." Tears welled up in Polly's eyes, "Will you ever come back?" Jake smiled, "It's a possibility…a real possibility."

A voice from the fog called, "Jake." It got louder until Jake was awake. Anne smiled, "I hated to wake you, honey, but it's time for us to go to bed…You looked like you were having a pleasant dream. At least you were smiling. What were you dreaming about?" Jake paused before answering. He mumbled, "Uhh, Anne, you know how dreams are. They're hard to remember…Bed sounds good to me."

From time to time Jake had wondered how life turned out for Polly. In the end it made no difference. Jake considered Anne, Caleb Burk, Burk Burnett and the Four-Sixes. There wasn't anything he would change about his current life.

Red Elk had counseled, "White Wolf, you will have many paths in your life. Accept the choices you make. That is the way of a true Comanche."

The End

859·245·3620

Jetson HAZE ELET

Made in United States
North Haven, CT
31 January 2023